# THE DAY OF THE DINOSAURS

# THE DAY OF THE DINOSAURS

*by*
*Eve Bunting*

*illustrated by*
*Judith Leo*

EMC Corporation, St. Paul, Minnesota

Library of Congress Cataloging in Publication Data

Bunting, Anne Eve.
    The day of the dinosaurs

    (The Dinosaur machines)
    SUMMARY: When one of them pulls the lever on the museum's dinosaur
display, three children are transported back to a prehistoric dinosaur land.
    [1. Dinosaurs—Fiction. 2. Space and time—Fiction] I. Leo, Judith. II. Title.
PZ7.B91527In                          [Fic]                          75-19023
ISBN 0-88436-193-4
ISBN 0-88436-194-2 pbk.

Published by EMC Corporation
180 East Sixth Street
St. Paul, Minnesota 55101
Printed in the United States of America

09876543

# THE DINOSAUR MACHINES

*The Day of the Dinosaurs*
*Escape from Tyrannosaurus*
*The Dinosaur Trap*
*Death of a Dinosaur*

Miss Wilson's class stood around the dinosaur display. Joe was in the front, next to the railing. Excitement fluttered inside him. This was the day he'd been waiting for.

"We call this the Triassic Period," the museum guide said. "The creatures you see here were alive 180 million years ago. Now watch."

He pulled a lever and the big, plastic dinosaurs began to move. They jerked and shook. Their mouths opened and closed.

"Get a look at the crocodile," Riley Brown said.

"It's not a crocodile," Joe muttered. "It's a phytosaur."

Big, dumb old Riley didn't hear him. If he had he'd probably have said, "Listen to Joe Know-it-all," in that sneery voice of his.

Today Joe had promised himself he wouldn't say one single word about dinosaurs. But it was pretty hard not to when he was bursting with information.

"What's the name of the big one at the back?" someone asked the guide.

Joe bit back the answer and let the guide tell.

"Plateosaurus. He was the largest of the very early dinosaurs."

"His bones were hollow," Joe said. He looked around secretly. Joe Know-it-all again! Lucky for him nobody was paying any attention.

The guide pushed down on the lever and the movement stopped.

"If you'll come over here you can see the plants of this period," he said.

Miss Wilson moved her class along behind him.

Joe straggled at the back. These were plants, not dinosaurs. He wasn't too interested. His eyes strayed to a brass plate on the wall. He read:

TO THE MEMORY
OF DR. HERMAN SMITH
WHO CREATED OUR
DINOSAUR DISPLAYS.

"I knew Herman."

Joe jumped. The voice seemed to come out of nowhere. He hadn't heard footsteps.

Standing beside him was an old man. He was
small and bent, and looked very frail in the long
dingy white lab coat he wore.

"Herman found the secret," the little man
whispered. "Herman could do wonderful
things—unearthly things." He began muttering to
himself. "Wouldn't tell me, wouldn't tell anyone.
Took the secret with him when he died. Selfish,
that's what Herman was." He was shouting now.
"But the dinosaurs know." His voice rang out,
cracking sharply, and people turned to look.

Joe began edging away. One of the museum guards came over. "Now Mr. Peters," he said gently. "You're acting up again."

Joe watched them disappear through the outside door. *Buggy,* he thought. *The poor old guy's buggy.*

The old cracked voice still rang in his mind. *"The dinosaurs know."*

What could plastic dinosaurs know about anything?

The rest of the class still stood around the plants. Joe shrugged and went on to the next dinosaur display.

Giant Brontosaurus stood on the edge of a fake lake. Allosaurus, the meat eater, was behind her.

Joe moved closer. Now he could see that there were two allosaurs, one in the front and another at the back. They looked real enough to smash down the railing, and lumber out into the room.

Carmen Garcia had left the rest of the class too. She stood alone, staring up at Brontosaurus. Carmen kept to herself a lot of the time. She didn't have many friends. She was too tough, too quick to talk back when she thought anyone was putting her down. Joe figured Carmen had to be tough. She lived in some kind of center where they put kids between foster homes. She'd told Joe once that she'd been in four foster homes and she'd run away from all of them. Once she'd made it all the way to the Mexican border.

Joe leaned on the railing beside her. Carmen pointed to the allosaur at the front.

"He looks just like my last foster father," she said. "Same teeth."

Joe grinned. "I don't blame you for getting out," he said.

A big bird turned lazily above Brontosaurus' head. Joe figured it must be on a wire.

Carmen pointed to it. "I bet that thing's really a piñata," she said. "I saw one just like it on Olivera Street."

"It's a pteranodon," Joe said. "Or maybe a Rhamphorhynchus."

The notice above the display said, "Jurassic Period."

Joe felt the excitement moving in him again. 150 million years ago these creatures were lords of the earth. Some day, some day Joe Lopez would be a dinosaur expert. He'd be a paleontologist, finding the big bones, putting the skeletons together. Once he'd told that to the class and everyone had laughed.

"Joe Know-it-all, Paleontologist," Riley Brown said.

Miss Wilson made Riley look the word up in the dictionary and tell the class exactly what it meant.

"A scientist who deals with the life of past geological periods based on the study of fossil remains of plants and animals," Riley read. "Wow, if you don't know it all now, Joe, you will then."

Of course that had been good for a laugh. Dumb, old Riley Brown who thought he was so great! Just because he was big, and good at sports and got picked first for everything.

Forget about Riley Brown, Joe told himself. Don't spoil today. It's dinosaur day.

He looked at Allosaurus. Allosaurus tore his prey apart with teeth and claw, ripping off hunks of flesh. His jaws could open real wide. Any animals small enough he could swallow whole. Joe shivered. Dinosaurs were the scariest things that had ever lived.

Again he seemed to hear the old voice. *"The dinosaurs know."* Know what? he wondered. Nothing that's what.

"Do these guys move too?" Riley Brown asked. He leaned across the railing beside Joe.

"I don't know," Joe said. He noticed that big, dumb old Riley didn't look so big next to the dinosaurs.

"I'll bet that's the lever." Riley reached over the railing and his feet lifted off the floor.

"Watch it," Joe said. He grabbed for Riley's leg and Carmen clutched at his arm. Riley toppled forward into the display. Joe had one quick glimpse of his hand closing around a piece of tree. Then he was falling forward too. And something was happening.

There was a great rush of wind. It was sucking him like an ant into a vacuum cleaner. He tried to hold on to the railing, but the railing wasn't there and his hands didn't seem to be there any more

either. He tried to yell, but no sound came out, not even a croak.

Then suddenly all was still and there was total silence.

Joe's eyes were tightly closed. He opened them and looked into sun so bright that it almost blinded him.

Riley was sprawled across the plastic plants and Joe was still holding his leg. Carmen still gripped his arm. Her blue dress was caught on a corner of one of the plants and she jerked it free, tearing a piece out.

''What happened?'' she gasped.

Joe and Riley stood up.

"We . . . we fell over the railing," Joe said. But already he knew it was more than that. Much more.

He looked around, his eyes slitted against the dazzle of the sun. How could sun be so bright all of a sudden? And where was the railing?

The display in front of him was bigger and had more depth. The air was hot and damp. The ferns by their feet were beaded with water. *It can't be,* he thought. *It can't be what I'm thinking.*

The big, grey body of Brontosaurus moved

slowly toward the lake. Her neck was like a thick, boneless snake swaying ahead of her.

Allosaurus stood upright, balanced on his tail. He was very still. *Waiting,* Joe thought dazedly. *Waiting and watching.*

The big killer lizard took a step forward. Carmen put a hand over her mouth. Her voice was muffled. "He moved."

"Well, I pulled the lever," Riley sounded uncertain, not a bit like himself. "It's not a real dinosaur. It's plastic."

The ferns that trembled under their feet weren't plastic. There was a small palm tree beside them. Joe touched its broad, flat leaf. It wasn't plastic either.

Allosaurus took another step. The sun shone on his red-brown hide. Spit hung from his half open mouth and his narrow eyes gleamed.

Over the thick beating of his own heart Joe could hear sounds. The slow unhurried thud of Brontosaurus' feet. Thunder Lizard, Joe thought. The thump of her feet was like the roll of distant thunder. Brontosaurus was real. Allosaurus was real too. Inside his head he heard again the old man in the museum. *"Herman could do wonderful things, unearthly things."*

"We came through a time barrier," Joe said. "We're back . . . back with the dinosaurs."

His voice was louder than he'd meant it to be. It hung in the air where no human voice had sounded before.

Allosaurus' heavy body turned toward them and they were fixed in his stare.

"Don't move," Joe whispered. "He doesn't know what we are. Stay still."

Brontosaurus' head snaked around. She saw Allosaurus. They could hear the terrified hiss of her

breath as she crashed through the swamp plants on the edge of the lake.

Allosaurus turned back to watch her. Then he was following her and he was faster than Joe would have believed possible.

He and Riley and Carmen edged slowly backward. All the time they watched Allosaurus, never taking their eyes from him for an instant. The strange tangle of ferns and roots were knee high. A small creature ran quickly past them. It looked like a plucked ostrich. Oviraptor, Joe thought. The egg eater.

They saw Brontosaurus smash into the lake. A wave, high as a wall rose on either side of her.

Allosaurus stopped as the water rushed over his feet. They could see the bulk of him, his neck and heavy legs; his tail that was flattened on the sides. He was big as a full grown tree. Then he turned and Joe saw his teeth. They were jagged as steak knives.

"He's seen us," Joe yelled. "Run! Run!"

They stumbled through the twisted underbrush. Roots twined around their legs and always, behind, they could hear the thump of the three-toed claws.

Riley stopped so suddenly that Joe and Carmen crashed into him.

Joe looked where his shaking finger pointed.

Another allosaur towered ahead of them.

"It's the one in the back of the display," Joe gasped. "I forgot about him." He'd been sitting there, watching, waiting for them to run into him. And they almost had.

In the silent world there was only the thud of the feet behind and their own shuddering breath. Then there was another sound. The thud of feet in front as the two killer lizards began to close in on them.

Joe looked desperately around. The lake and Brontosaurus, safe in its waters. "Quick!" Joe said. "We've got to cross between them and get into the lake. Allosaurus can't swim."

They had to circle so close to the one in front that Joe could see the rubbery shine of its hide. They ran so close that he could smell it. Old smell, earth smell, cage-in-the-zoo smell.

Now they were through them and the lake was only yards away. They were going to make it.

His foot caught in something and the jolt took the breath from him. He looked down. It was a skull . . . a small dinosaur skull, and his toe was stuck in the empty eye socket. Frantically he jerked it free, twisting it. Pain shot into his ankle. *Run,* he told himself, *run!*

The allosaurs were bigger than anything he'd ever seen, and they were coming, coming at him on two sides. *Run, Run,* he screamed inside, and he was trying to run, but he couldn't.

Carmen darted back. Her eyes were glazed and her hands plucked at him.

''It's no good,'' Joe gasped. ''You can't. Go on. Run.''

Then Riley was beside him. Joe saw the sweat of fear on his face. He reached out, and Riley's arm was under him, dragging him, half carrying him.

Then the ground was soft under their feet and the lake water lapped around their legs. Mud sucked at their shoes.

Riley stopped. "What if there are crocodiles? Or those other things that look like them."

Joe tried to speak through the pain. "I don't think so. We have to . . . take a chance."

They clung together. Riley and Carmen pulled Joe between them. When the water was chest high they stopped.

"Is this far enough?" Riley asked.

"They won't come in at all," Joe said. "We're safe here."

Brontosaurus' head snaked toward them and Carmen ducked.

"She only eats plants," Joe said.

"Yeah. But does she know I'm not a plant," Carmen muttered.

The two allosaurs glared across the water. Strings of spit, like cobwebs, hung from their open mouths. Their forelegs pawed the air. *THEY know we're meat,* Joe thought.

Carmen's voice was shaky. "Wow are they mad! No dinner today, you guys."

A strange mist drifted like smoke across the lake. Above them the sky was so blue that it hurt to look at it. *No smog,* Joe thought. *No cars, no people, just us. And it's 150 million years ago!*

Brontosaurus was like a big, grey castle, surrounded by a moat. They could hear the hiss of the water as her neck dipped in and out, pulling up plants.

"She doesn't even have the sense to be curious about us," Joe said. "Her brain weighs less than a pound."

Carmen shook her head. "I can't believe this. I can't believe any of it. How did it happen, Joe?"

"I was messing around as usual," Riley said. "And I pulled the wrong lever. It must have been some kind of time-reverse thing. The display was a dinosaur machine." He splashed at the water. "Why can't I just leave things alone?"

Joe looked up at him. "You didn't know." There was something else he had to say. "Thanks a whole lot for coming back for me."

"A good thing he did," Carmen said. "I always figured I was pretty strong, but I wasn't strong enough. You sure are, Riley."

"Yeah." Riley nodded toward Brontosaurus. "Big and strong and stupid, like her."

Joe couldn't believe this was Riley Brown talking. Riley Brown who was always so sure of himself.

Carmen's eyes never left the two allosaurs who sat unmoving on the shore. "Give up," she said. "Come on . . . give up! Disappear."

"They'll have to sooner or later," Joe said. "Then we'll look for the lever. Let's hope it works the other way around."

"If it doesn't . . ." Riley left the sentence unfinished.

Joe moved his hurt foot gently in the water. Something touched his leg and his heart raced. It was a piece of trailing plant, like seaweed. He let it float away. It would be nice to know for sure that there were no crocodiles. He looked past the two killer lizards at the strange, swampy greenness. The feeling of wonder was stronger than his fear. Things no human had ever seen before. Air no human had ever breathed.

"We could probably stay alive if we had to," he said. "We could make knives and build a house. There'd be plants to eat, and game. We could make a fire."

They stood silently in the water.

"For sure the social worker would never find me here," Carmen said at last. There was a strange, far away look on her face.

"Why do you run away?" Riley asked.

"I don't know. I don't like it where I am . . . ever. Someday I'll get to Mexico. Mexico will be different."

"Different how?" Joe asked. He wanted to say, "they've got foster homes there too, and probably places just like the center."

Carmen shrugged. "It has to be different."

A bird swooped low. It had a long tail and they could see scales on its legs.

"Rhamphorynchus," Joe said. "Fish eater. It wasn't a piñata after all, Carmen."

"You sure are smart," Riley said softly and Joe looked at him quickly. But somehow Riley's voice didn't sound the way it used to.

"I'm only smart about dinosaurs," he said.

"No, about a lot of things. I always wanted to be you, knowing the right answers. Maybe that's why ..." His voice trailed away.

"You wanted to be me?" Joe shook his head. "Naw it was the other way around. I wanted to be like you."

"Don't worry about it," Carmen said. "Some days I want to be Sharon Johnson and some days I want to be Penny Lane. Mostly I just want to be anybody but me."

*Yeah,* Joe thought, *I bet you do too.* He wriggled his ankle. It was weird standing here, knowing where they were and that maybe they would never get out and talking about things like this. Things that weren't really important, compared to living and dying. But what else was there to talk about except themselves and the world they knew?

"When we get back," he said, "I'll show you the brass plate in honor of Herman."

"Who's Herman?" Carmen asked.

"A friend of Mr. Peters," Joe said. Mr. Peters, who wasn't so buggy after all.

The sun beat down on their heads and the air was clammy. It felt like a shower stall after you turn off the hot water.

"Look," Carmen said. "They're going."

The two big meat eaters clumped through the thick mass of plants.

"After they feed they'll sleep for a week or two," Joe said.

"Well let's not wait till then," Riley muttered. "Let's find that lever."

They watched till the big, blunted heads were almost lost in the distance. Then they splashed out.

There were allosaur prints in the soft mud. They looked like the claw marks of giant, heavy birds.

Riley looked around. "Where do we start? There's no way to tell where we came in."

"Yes there is," Carmen pointed. A scrap of blue was caught on a spiky plant. It was the only blue under the blue of the sky. "My dress," she said, "where I tore it."

Joe hopped as quickly as he could behind them. If dinosaurs could think, reason, what would they make of their human prints in the mud?

Carmen plucked the piece of blue from the bladed plant and they got down on their knees and began searching. There were all kinds of roots and twisted branches.

"Wait a minute," Joe said. "We were touching when we came through the time barrier. We'd better be touching when we go back. If we don't, maybe we won't go together."

They stared at each other. How would it feel to be left behind? Quickly they joined hands and began again to search. Joe didn't know which of them found the lever and pulled it.

One moment they were in the world of the dinosaurs, the next they were back in the museum. There had been a whoosh of hot wind, like standing behind a jet plane at take-off. When he opened his eyes he knew they were back.

"You three," Miss Wilson said. "Don't lean across the railing. It's put there so we know to stay on this side."

Joe's eyes met Riley's and slid away. Had he imagined it all? Or was time then much longer than time here and now?

Carmen nudged him and opened her hand. Crumpled inside was the scrap of blue.

Miss Wilson glared down at their feet. "Mud all over your shoes. And why are you limping, Joe Lopez? I thought you were interested in dinosaurs."

"He is," Riley said. "He knows all about them and it comes in pretty useful."

"Allosaurus can't swim," Carmen said.

"And Brontosaurus only eats plants," Riley added.

"But I've got to look up about the crocodiles," Joe said.

Miss Wilson stared at them as if they'd gone crazy. "Keep with the rest of the class now," she said. The three of them dropped back a little.

34

"Let's not tell anyone," Carmen said. She had that strange far away look on her face again.

Riley nodded. "They'd think we were bananas."

The museum guide pulled a lever. It wasn't the one Riley had pulled.

Allosaurus took one jerky stride toward the lake.

Carmen's nails dug into Joe's arm.

"Allosaurus was slow and clumsy," the guide began.

"Uh-uh," Joe said. "He could move pretty fast."

Someone sniggered, "Joe Know-it-all knows it all."

Riley pushed forward. His fists were clenched. "Clam up on the Joe Know-it-all stuff," he said. "Just because you're a bunch of dum-dums."

"Now, now," Miss Wilson said.

Riley stepped back again between Joe and Carmen. They were suddenly a unit, the three of them, with things shared that no one knew about.

"Man, that was really neat," Riley whispered. "I mean, now that it's over, I'm glad it happened. Aren't you?"

Joe scraped mud from his shoe and rubbed it between his fingers. Prehistoric dirt. What would a lab make of it? He wished he'd brought back samples of the plants.

"We could probably go again," Riley said. "Maybe even into a different display. If there's one lever there may be others. And next time we'd be sure to tie something on it so we could find it easily."

"And we'd take bottles and stuff and bring things back," Joe said. "And a camera. Can you believe dinosaur pictures?"

He heard Carmen draw in her breath. "Maybe
we could build that house you were talking about,
Joe."

"The Swiss Family Robinson in Dinosaur
Land," Riley said.

Joe looked along the row of displays. Had
Herman turned all of them into dinosaur machines?
Next time it would be smart to pick one with no
meat-eaters in it.

"It would be like having our own world," Carmen said. "Nobody to hassle us. Nobody to tell us what to do."

"It would be crazy," Joe muttered. But his heart was pounding and already he knew. For their own reasons they all wanted to go back. The only question left was when.

ting, Anne Eve.

day of the
nosaurs